The Year the Raiders Came

M. A. Wood

**Illustrated by
Chris Mara**

Byways

The Year the Raiders Came

First published by Andersen Press Limited,
London, in 1977.

Paperback edition first published 1983 by
Byway Books, 9 Maxton Court, Hawick,
Roxburghshire TD9 7QN.

©   Text 1977 M.A. Wood
©   Illustrations 1983 Byway Books

ISBN 0 907448 07 0

Photo Typeset by Print Origination, Bootle,
Merseyside L20 6NS.
Printed in Scotland by Kelso Graphics, The
Knowes, Kelso, Roxburghshire.

**This book is published with the financial assistance of the
Scottish Arts Council**

Contents

One : The Flock-gathering

St Mary's Abbey looked very peaceful in the bright May morning, with the great central tower of the cross-shaped church rising high above the rest of the monastery buildings where the white-robed monks were going about their tasks with quiet concentration.

Round one side of the Abbey the muddy River Waver wound its slow way to the sea, and on the other side lay the meadows where the villagers kept their cattle and the huge, fertile, open fields with their strips of oats, barley and fallow making a pattern of green and brown. Over the centuries the monks had reclaimed these fields from the vast forests covering most of northern England, till they looked so like a large well-tended garden that travellers through the wild Border Marches—the borders of England and Scotland—called it 'the cultivated place', which the monks in their Latin speech changed to Holm Cultram.

The little village just outside the red sandstone walls of the Abbey was quiet too that morning—unusually so. The women, who generally worked hard in the fields alongside their menfolk, were standing at the doors of their white-washed clay cottages enjoying a good gossip, though some of the more industrious ones had their hands busy with distaff and spindle at the same time. Beside them the babies lay in oval wickerwork baskets and the toddlers played happily in the dust with none of the older children to disturb their games.

They were all down at the sheep pens beside the track leading to the estuary marshes where everything was bustle and confusion. The air rang with the bleating of frightened sheep, the barking of dogs, excited shouts from men and children, and above all the harsh voice of Flockmaster, the burly, uncouth head shepherd, swearing at everyone and using his stick on animals and children alike—especially on his little, orphan herd boy, David.

The tides were rising as they did with every turn of the moon, and the monastery sheep which grazed on the crisp, salty turf round the mouth of the river, had to be brought to safe ground before the grass was covered with flood water. It was also the most important flock-gathering of the year, for the sheep were about to be clipped and on the sale of their wool depended the prosperity of the Abbey.

So they were being counted into their pens and the numbers checked off on wooden tally sticks, just as Brother Dominic, the most unpopular of the brethren, arrived with a companion to see that everything was done correctly.

'Boy!' he demanded, catching sight of David who had just received a particularly severe cut from Flockmaster's stick, 'What have you done to merit such chastisement?'

David straightened his thin, aching body and looked up at the grave faces above him. He knew the village and the land about it belonged to the Abbey, and that he and the other people who worked on that land were servants of the monks. But why, oh why did Brother Dominic have to come along at this time? If only gentle Brother John, standing as usual a pace in the background, had been alone.

'I've not done anything.' David returned the monk's frown with a steadfast gaze. It wasn't his fault that one of the sheep was missing. Like the rest of the village boys, David had been running and scrambling about on the marsh since daybreak, and he had done his best to keep up with the others, mostly bigger than himself. But their breakfast had been rye bread and cheese, David's had only been a dry crust.

'Not done anything? Do not add falsehood to your sins,' the stern voice thundered above him.

The men and youths who had been occupied with the sheep began crowding round. It was always entertaining to hear Brother Dominic scolding someone—as long as you weren't the culprit!

'He's lost one of my best sheep, your reverence,' said Flockmaster in the smarmy tones he always used to address the monks, 'as fine a young gimmer (young ewe) as the Abbey possesses. Would have had twin lambs next spring, I shouldn't wonder. My lad, Garath, told him to go back and fetch it.' So it was Garath who had got him into trouble, thought David, he might have guessed it.

'But,' Flockmaster was continuing, 'the lazy brat didn't bother himself.'

'Is this true?' boomed Brother Dominic, 'You have neglected your duties to the extent of allowing the monastery which has fed, clothed and cared for you since you were a babe, to lose a valuable animal? Are you not aware how this holy foundation depends on the sale of our wool and that even now merchants in Europe are waiting impatiently for the next consignment? And YOU, you miserable waif, have lost us a sheep!'

David didn't reply. What was the use?

'Go back to the marsh at once and redeem your error. Find that sheep!'

Hopelessly David turned away. Back across that lonely wind-swept waste. He shivered as he thought about it.

'Stay a moment,' the second monk moved forward, 'Could the boy not have a companion in his trial, Brother? He is only a child yet, and the sheep may be difficult to catch. Here you!' Glancing round the crowd, he beckoned a sturdy boy some two years older than David and with a cheery, round face. 'You're Robin Skelton aren't you? Our good joiner's son. Well, go with David, Robin, and help him find this sheep.'

Then with a sideways look at Brother Dominic who had moved away with the other men to study the animals in their brushwood sheep-pens, he whisked a couple of rather wizened apples from somewhere under his habit and pressed them into the boys' hands. 'I dare say you hadn't much to eat this morning, David. Now off you go and God bless you!'

With grateful 'thank you's' the boys hurried away till they were out of sight of the crowd. Then they walked slower and Robin polished his apple on his tunic to postpone the delicious moment of sinking his teeth in it.

'What a pity they're so small,' he remarked, 'and of course, the best will have gone for My Lord Abbot's table long ago. We're lucky to taste them so late in the season—but it was good of Brother John.'

'Oh, it was!' agreed David, remembering many other little kindnesses, and especially how Brother John had explained to him about his name.

When David had been found as a tiny

baby, abandoned beside the old Norman door of the Abbey, the good fathers had christened the child after two very important people: the saintly Scottish king, David the First, who endowed their monastery in the far off happy days when there was no fighting between England and Scotland; and holy David in scripture, who wrote the psalms and rose from being a humble shepherd to a mighty ruler.

'Do you know, David,' Robin's voice broke in on his thoughts, 'my father says a day will come when we won't all have to obey the monks. Somebody told him that away abroad—in Germany I think it is—there's a man called Martin Luther who makes out everyone has a right to read the Bible in their own language, and he writes books about a whole lot of other things the Church is wrong about.'

'Oh, how wicked!' gasped David. 'He must be the devil himself.'

Robin laughed. 'Oh, I don't think so, but don't worry. It's maybe just a story.'

They went on crunching their apples for a few more minutes. Though wrinkle-skinned, the fruit was quite whole and had a sweet

tang to it. As he spat out the core, Robin spoke again. 'Do you like working with the sheep, David?'

'No, I don't,' said David decidedly. He hated sheep, the smell of their oily wool, the maggots that bred in their fleeces, and the tar used for dressing their sores. 'I wish I could be apprenticed to your father,' he added wistfully.

'I wish you could too. I showed him those little figures you carved and he said you were a born wood-worker.'

'Isn't it strange,' Robin went on thoughtfully, 'how we always want to do something different? I'm supposed to be smoothing boards this morning, but I was sick of being covered with wood shavings and ran away to help with the sheep. I'll get a good hiding too when I go back.'

David smiled to himself. Robin was a spoilt only son, not a waif who'd been left at the church door in a leather bag. *His* punishment was not likely to be severe.

Soon the boys left the track they had been following and came to the saltings where the flock grazed. It was a great grassy plain and now there were no people, dogs or sheep rushing about on it, David thought the marsh looked very lonely and frightening.

But the River Waver was there, lazily flowing through the grassland, and Robin cast an experienced glance at the water.

'It's going the right way,' he said, 'we're safe for a while.'

David nodded. He too, knew they were safe till the high tide in the Solway Firth several miles away forced the river water to run backward till it overflowed the banks and covered the grass.

'Look,' went on Robin as they paused to stare hopelessly across the empty space, 'the flock were driven in this direction, so that cursed animal must be down in one of the creeks. Well, what do you say if we separate and each follow a different creek to the riverside. Then whoever first spots the sheep can give a good whistle.' He put two fingers in his mouth and blew shrilly. It was an accomplishment the village boys were very proud of.

'All right,' agreed David, and they began their weary trudge. Along the creek banks they went, looking anxiously at every ledge of turf where the sheep might be standing, hidden from the view of anyone out on the marsh.

Back and forwards they tramped. David's legs grew tired, his shoulders stiff, his head throbbed, and his inside felt strangely hollow.

At first the boys had kept waving gaily to each other but as time went on David just couldn't be bothered. The driftwood in the creeks and his own shadow on the grass seemed to flicker and grow dim. What would happen, he wondered dully, if night came before they found the sheep.

Something moved down at the mouth of a creek. Were his eyes playing tricks? He blinked and stared harder. Yes, there it was! Sitting on the sand, a dirty grey heap, almost indistinguishable from the mud around it.

He scrambled down and looked closer. To his dismay he found it was not sitting but resting in a pool of liquid mud caused by its efforts to get free from what was obviously a quicksand. Struggling had merely worked it deeper into the ooze and now the water was lapping its body. Whatever could they do to get it out?

'Ah, you've found it!' Robin's bright face

peered over the edge of the creek. 'I thought you must have when I saw you disappear.' He lowered himself to David's side. 'Holy Mary! What a mess! That one's properly mired down.'

'What shall we do?' asked David. He felt a little better. His eyes seemed to be clearer since he had stood still and his brain was beginning to work again.

'Do?' Robin gave a short laugh. 'We'd never get her out of that without men and ropes . . . I tell you what, we'll just go home and say we found her lying dead.'

'Oh no,' cried David, 'we couldn't tell a lie to Brother Dominic. Besides Flockmaster said it was so valuable.'

'Valuable! That one!' laughed Robin loudly, 'Oh nonsense! Look at that wool, I'm sure it's poor quality. Don't you see, David, Flockmaster was just putting the blame on you to cover his own carelessness. You know he should have checked all the flock himself instead of leaving those last two pens to Garath. Besides he was sucking up to Brother Dominic.'

David sat down quickly on a tussock of grass. His legs felt weak again. Perhaps it was at hearing such astonishing ideas. He'd not thought of a grown-up being deceitful before, especially not the man he had been taught to consider as his master.

'If you don't like telling lies,' Robin was saying, 'just wait till I find a post and I'll knock the old ewe on the head for you.'

He began to search along the tide-line.

'Oh no! Don't do that! I'll come back with you.'

Perhaps, David thought, somebody *might* rescue it later.

As the boys climbed out of the hollow and started on their slow way homeward, the sheep, realizing it was being abandoned, gave a feeble, despairing bleat.

David turned back. The animal seemed to be crying for help.

'I can't go with you,' he said abruptly. 'I can't leave it.'

'Don't be daft!' retorted Robin. 'What good can you do? And you needn't think I'm going to tell anyone and come dragging all this way back again. I'll want my supper by the time I get home.'

'I'm staying,' repeated David firmly, and slipped down over the creek side once more.

He could hear Robin's retreating footsteps growing fainter as the older boy moved away. David seated himself on the tussock he'd occupied before and stared at the sheep. It blinked its almond-shaped eyes and seemed to stare back.

'Poor sheep, we're both the same,' David told it, 'nobody wants us. Nobody cares if we're dead or alive. Your wool isn't good enough and I'm too small to work properly. So no one minds what happens to us. We're no use at all. Perhaps it would be better if we both died.'

David sniffed a little. He knew he was nearly too big to cry but he felt very like it, especially when he thought of Robin, safe in his parents' comfortable cottage, sitting down to a good hot meal. David wondered what it would be, rabbit stew perhaps. The joiner's grateful customers sometimes paid him with a coney (rabbit) or two.

Flockmaster's six hungry, selfish children would be crowding in too for their usual fare of watery onion broth, and though David should be among them it was most likely none would bother even to ask where he was.

A terrible loneliness came over him. It

wasn't caused by the vast, silent marsh around, but by the memory of the many times Flockmaster had punished him unjustly, and the way the other children had often refused to let him join in their games. Nobody in the village wanted to partner David the foundling. Except occasionally Robin. Sometimes Robin had forcefully told the others to let him play with them; and once when David was quite little, he'd actually fought Garath because that bully had set one of the bull-baiting dogs on the younger boy.

Yes, Robin *was* kind, and when he got over his temper he'd be sure to tell someone about David and the sheep. It was just a matter of waiting.

The animal turned its head restlessly from side to side. 'Are you tired of being there?' asked David. 'I know! I'll sing to you to make the time pass quicker.'

Shifting his painful body to an easier position on the sand, he considered what it should be. One of the glees they sang at Christmas? The psalms he'd heard at the Abbey? Yes, *The Lord is My Shepherd*. The very thing! He'd sing that. It was difficult to manage the Latin words but after a few false starts he thought he'd got it right; and the sheep kept quite still as if it were comforted too. David wondered if David the shepherd in the scriptures, often sang to himself when he was sitting alone with his charges on the hillside in Palestine.

He felt so pleased with his effort he tried a few more familiar psalms, but they weren't quite as good. So he sang the villager's harvest supper song and a Christmas carol.

By then the sun had slanted round so that its warmth was full on him, his weary body nestled snugly against the sand, and slowly David's eyelids drooped till he was sound asleep.

When he woke he was cold and stiff. A thin, chill breeze was blowing across the marsh, and the sunlight had moved once more, leaving his hollow in shade. It must be nearly time for evening service.

He looked at the sheep. It seemed deeper in the mud than before—or was there more water in the creek?

Yes, it certainly seemed deeper, and as he watched the animal slipped sideways, letting its head flop till it was almost in the water.

'Oh sheep, don't drown before they come!' cried David desperately. 'Oh, what shall I do? I know! I'll have to try and hold your head up.'

With that he stepped out on to the mud as close to the sheep as he dared. It was too near. The quicksand closed round his legs, making him feel like a fly caught in honey. It was VERY frightening!

'Now I'm stuck! It's all your fault, you silly old yow (ewe). Keep your stupid head up, can't you!'

He grasped the sheep's face with both hands and pointed it firmly skyward. Then he looked again at the water. There was definitely more. In fact it was bubbling up the creek quite quickly. He watched it soaking through the sheep's wool, and as it did so the animal appeared to rise slightly as if it were about to float. David too, felt his feet rather freer as the incoming water stirred the mud.

But the tide was still rising. They were both going to be drowned! Screaming wildly, David tried to help himself, throwing his body about in all directions, but it was no use. In his panic he only worked himself nearer to the sheep and deeper into the mire.

His ragged tunic was completely soaked, he could hardly maintain his balance, and he only saved himself from falling face downwards by clasping the sheep's neck. He clung to it, sobbing in despair, as the water rose and rose.

He was just wondering in a terrified sort of way, if it wouldn't be easier to let go of the sheep's head which he was still trying to keep straight up, and allow both of them to sink into the frothing water, when suddenly it stopped rising. Actually stopped! A few inches below the sheep's nose. David could hardly believe his eyes. He watched it steadily for what seemed like hours, and then, as suddenly as it had risen, the water began to drop again.

They were SAFE! David gave a little moan of relief, and slipped down in a dead faint with his head resting on the sheep's back.

What was happening, thought David in bewilderment? He was sitting on something soft, warm—and dry! There was a faint perfume in the air too. A strange, sharp odour he seemed to know. Incense! The incense he'd smelt so often in the great church. But he was on the marsh—or was he? Somebody was trying to pour wine into his mouth. Perhaps he was dead and having Holy Communion in heaven with the angels. Blessed Saints! He must see what it was like!

David opened his eyes and looked straight up at the kindly, weather-beaten face of Brother John. The monk smiled and so did David. 'The—the apples were good, Father,' he said faintly.

'Poor child,' Brother John spoke tenderly.

'Here Robin, he's coming to. You support him while I bring another cloak from the pack-mules.'

David felt better. 'What's happening?' He was aware of more voices nearby. 'Where's the sheep?'

'Why see,' said Robin, helping him sit up, 'they're getting it out now. And just look at Brother Dominic!'

Turning his head David saw there were a group of villagers standing on the edge of the creek—Flockmaster was not among them. Some were holding ropes, others bundles of straw. Down in the mud a man was busy digging out the sheep with his bare hands while another spread straw around them to make a firm basis to work on. But the most surprising thing was that Brother Dominic was sitting in the mud too, with his habit all sodden and a big streak of dirt across his face. While most surprising of all, he was actually supporting the sheep's head and looking into its slanting eyes with an expression of unusual gentleness. Brother Dominic who'd never been known to smile at a baby or stroke a dog!

Robin chuckled. 'Doesn't he look funny? He's doing penance for sending you back, David. We all thought you'd be drowned when we got here. Brother John says it may be a miracle—and there hasn't been one at the Abbey for over a hundred years.'

'How did they know where I was?' asked David.

'Oh, I had to tell them,' Robin admitted— David knew he would. 'I couldn't eat my supper for thinking of you out here alone. Brother John gave me such a scolding.' He grimaced ruefully.

'He said I was just like the hireling in the scripture story who ran away. But David, I told him how you don't like working with the sheep and they're going to let Father teach you woodwork instead. And you've to live in our house now, David—Mother says so—we're going to share the loft. Won't that be grand? We'll have some fine fun together!'

'Oh yes, but—but Flockmaster—' David went all shivery again as he suddenly remembered his cruel guardian. 'Will—will he let me?'

'Oh David, don't be daft! It's all right—all right, I tell you! Brother John's settled Flockmaster. Didn't I say? I'd never seen him so angry before? You've abused that boy long enough, shepherd, he told him, if by God's mercy we find him still alive, he leaves your charge at once! Oh David, you should have seen Flockmaster's face, he slunk off like one of his own dogs. You know, at first I believe he thought you'd work with us during the day and still run about for him in your free time—but hush! Here's Brother John coming back.'

He broke off quickly as the monk returned to them.

'Well David, how do you feel now, child? Better? That's right.' He bent over David, wrapped the extra cloak round him, and, picking up the boy, carried him towards the pack-mules. 'It's time we got you home now. I suppose Robin will have told you all our plans. Do they make you happy, little good shepherd?'

'Oh yes,' said David with a contented sigh, 'very happy.'

But as David rode joyfully through the village to his new life, Flockmaster's family in their dirty hut beside the sheep-pens were listening to the head shepherd's grumbles.

'They've gone and given the boy to Joiner Skelton,' he said. 'Why should he have a new apprentice? The fellow's always getting favours. It was only last week when we had our archery practice they put him into my place as head of our division.'

'Well, you stopped too long at the ale-house,' grunted his eldest son, Garath, who was sprawled at full length on the heap of rushes which served his parents as a bed. 'Captain said you couldn't be relied on.'

'And it's a wonder you weren't with me!' retorted his father. 'The practices are a waste of time anyway. The Scots never come this far nowadays. But I'll get even with Skelton—see if I don't!'

'They all think they're a cut above us,' said Flockmaster's wife. 'Look at the way she dresses that Robin. I've heard say Master Skelton can read too. Maybe that's why he gets in with the monks.'

'Nonsense, lass! Only priests and heretics reads—but somebody once said they'd seen the packman fetch him a parcel—I wonder what was in it . . . '

'Oh well, never mind now,' Flockmaster's wife was tired of the conversation, 'Let's have our suppers. There'll be more scraps for the dogs now that boy's away.'

Two : The Raid

It was a lovely day in late summer, the harvest had been safely gathered in, and Lammas, the Loaf Mass, celebrated several weeks before. The sunlight shone through the open door of Master Skelton's workshop and made glittering patterns on the bright steel of the saws and other tools hanging on the wall.

David would learn to handle those saws when he was big enough, but meantime his immediate task was to shape each of the small lengths of wood in the heap beside him into pegs for fastening larger pieces of timber together.

Nobody could call it really interesting work, and sometimes—but only some-times—on days like this when he was cooped up in the hot, dusty workshop, David thought rather wistfully of his former open air life out in the fields with the other village children: perhaps tossing the sweet-scented hay till it was dry enough to be stacked for winter; or gleaning the last precious grains of corn from among the golden stubble.

Wearily, David threw down another finished peg. It was really too bad of Robin not to be here helping, but since he'd come to live at the joiner's, David couldn't help noticing that Robin was deserting his work more and more frequently. In fact whenever his father's back was turned, and he was relying on David to complete any neglected jobs before Master Skelton noticed. The joiner, though a kind, easy-going man, took a great pride in his trade and wouldn't tolerate slipshod work even from his own son.

Not that David really minded helping Robin. When he thought about the wonderful change that had taken place in his life, he couldn't object to anything.

How he loved the warm, dry attic above the other two rooms of the house where he and Robin slept on separate palliasses of clean, soft hay. So different from lying on the earth floor among Flockmaster's rough, smelly children who kicked and pinched if they imagined anyone was getting more than his fair share of room—and this generally meant David.

It had been difficult to get used to such luxury at first, and several times David had dreamt he saw Flockmaster's cruel, unshaven face with its cold, cunning grey eyes, bending over him—and that horrible stick upraised.

Several times he woke from these dreams sweating with fear. And he remembered that just after he'd left Flockmaster's, one of the boys he knew, whose father kept the ale-house, had told him that the head shepherd was always making threats against Master Skelton.

But these fears were gradually fading from David's mind. Big, strong, clever Master Skelton could surely look after himself—and his new apprentice too. David had complete faith in his master, and at the joiner's house there was so much to learn and enjoy.

It was grand to be always clean for one thing! Robin's mother insisted they changed the hay in their bedding regularly, and every morning made each of them draw a bucket of water from the well to wash with. When he was at Flockmaster's, David had been filthy all the time—and hungry too. The scrapings of the porridge pot and any other leftover food had been his usual meals.

Mistress Skelton made the crispest and sweetest oatcakes in the north of England—as her husband often told her—and David had never tasted anything so good before. Her broth too, was delicious, thick with peas and beans and flavoured with her own special mixture of herbs. She always ladled out an extra helping into David's bowl, saying with a smile: 'You can't work if you don't eat!' David could almost feel himself growing fatter day by day.

Mistress Skelton had also declared she wasn't going to have a boy going in and out of *her* house dressed in rags. So she'd woven a length of cloth from the wool of the local sheep, called Herdwicks, and made David a smart slate-grey tunic which would stand up to any amount of hard wear.

When he first put it on he almost wondered if he were the same person and felt nearly too shy to go through the village. But except for Garath's young brothers and a few of their unpleasant playmates, who shouted, 'How's Lord Muck today?', 'Thinks he's too good for us now!' and threatened to throw stones, nobody else showed much surprise. Indeed many of the grown-ups smiled approvingly at him and said how smart he looked.

'David! David! What do you think!' it was Robin's voice, and David looked up to see his friend, red-faced and breathing hard, coming into the workshop. 'I've such news! There's going to be a raid!'

'A RAID!'

'Yes, a raid! isn't it exciting? Everybody's talking about it. I'm off to hear some more.'

David sat blindly looking at the work before him. A raid! How awful! Though he lived so near Scotland he couldn't remember there having been a raid before. Their little village, by the walls of the great monastery, was rather out of the path of the northern raiders, who when they came burning and fighting into the Western Marches of England, seldom got past the garrison city of Carlisle. But David had often heard older people describing raids that had taken place in the past and the terrible deeds done then. Yet in spite of seeing the village men practising drilling and archery every week, and listening to the big boys boasting about what *they* would do if the wicked Scots ever came anywhere near, David had never really thought it could happen. What would a Scot look like, he wondered. He'd never seen one.

'David!' It was Mistress Skelton this time. 'Ah, there you are. Still at work like a good boy. I saw Robin dashing out of the garden. I suppose he told you there was going to be a raid? We must prepare at once.'

David saw her rosy, pleasant face was pale and anxious. 'Is—is it really true, Mistress?'

'Oh, I'm afraid so, David. A man has just ridden by to say a band of Scots crossed the Solway at low tide this morning and were moving in this direction. Oh dear, as soon as the autumn nights draw in I live in fear of raids—but at least they're coming by daylight this time.'

'Mother!' Robin was back. 'Just listen! They say the Scots are only five miles off and burning all the houses. They're led by Nebless Nick!'

'Nebless Nick! Holy Virgin protect us!'

Mistress Skelton sounded really frightened. Nebless (Nose-less) Nick Armstrong was a fearsome man whose nose had been slashed by a sword cut, and he was the raider about whom all the worst and most horrifying tales were told.

'I wonder if there'll be any fighting here.'

Robin picked up a chisel and brandished it like a dagger.

'Now Robin, don't be foolish! Your father's away to the muster, to band together with the other men, and I've only you boys to help me. What have we been told to do if there was a raid?'

'Collect our tools and pack them carefully in wool so that they don't get damp or blunt,' recited the boys together.

'That's it. The tools first for they are our livelihood—though who'll use them if anything happens to your father I don't know . . . ' she added half to herself. 'Then take and hide all the things you're making and as much of the best wood as you can, in case they fire the workshop. I'll collect the household goods—but hurry, for we must take shelter in the Abbey as soon as the bell begins to ring.'

She turned away and the boys began putting the valuable tools into sacks of waste wool which prudent Master Skelton had kept ready for just such an emergency. Then they carried all the finest quality timber as well as the stools, troughs, cattle yokes, and other partly-finished work, out through the cottage garden and concealed them among the bushes on the waste land nearby.

'Couldn't I just take my knights with us?' begged Robin as they ran into the kitchen. This wooden model of two jousting knights, who moved when you pulled strings, was Robin's greatest treasure. His father had made it for him years before, and the boys always played with it if the weather was bad and work slack. He was reluctant to leave it hidden in the gorse. David had nothing of his own except his new tunic and a good knife which one of the village men had given him after the rescue of the sheep.

'Take a toy? Of course not!' Mistress Skelton was cross. 'We've quite enough to carry. Come here!'

She had packed their few clothes and bedcoverings into neat bundles with her pots and pans inside, so she fastened the smallest bundle on David's back and gave him a basket of food to carry. Robin took the next largest and one of the bags of tools.

'Now,' said his mother, hoisting her own bundle on her shoulders, 'we've just the pig to get.'

She led the way to the sty at the far side of

her garden. The pig was the only animal they had to bother about, for Master Skelton's two cows were out in the common pasture in charge of the village herd who would be responsible for the safety of all the cattle.

'Listen, there's the warning bell! We must be within the gates before it stops.' She glanced sadly round her little garden with its beds of bright flowers of which she was so proud, the vegetable patch with tidy rows of cabbages, onions, and radishes, and the straw bee hives standing on little wooden platforms at the very end of the garden. David imagined she must be wondering what it would be like when they came back and he noticed there were tears in her eyes as she quickly turned her head away.

The joiner's house stood away from the other cottages at the end of the village furthest from the Abbey, and they soon joined a stream of women and children who were also hurrying there for refuge. Some of them were helping along aged relations, others were carrying babies or baskets of squawking fowls in addition to their other burdens.

They had almost reached the main gate of the Abbey and the men on the watch towers at either side of it were shouting to them to make haste, when Mistress Skelton suddenly stopped.

'Oh, Our Blessed Lady forgive me!' she cried, 'I've forgotten the little coffer with the money in it. Oh, what shall we do? Your father will be so angry.'

The boys knew the box she was talking about. It stood on a high shelf in the bedroom and contained several small bags of coins— the joiner's life savings. The villagers so seldom used money that Mistress Skelton had easily overlooked it in the excitement.

'I'll soon run back for it!' exclaimed Robin.

'No, I will,' said David, 'you need Robin to help you, Mistress.'

'I need you both.' Mistress Skelton was upset. 'I can't carry everything myself. Oh, is there no one who could aid us?'

She looked at the groups of anxious people around them. But they were all too busy trying to save themselves and their possessions to notice the Skeltons' predicament. Then Mistress Skelton's face lightened as she caught sight of a tall, ungainly man who was walking a little apart from the others. He was dressed in rags and carried a three-legged stool upside down on his head. 'Gowkie Graeme!' she gasped with relief. 'He'll do.'

Gowkie Graeme was a poor half-witted creature who did odd jobs about the village because he couldn't be trusted with proper work. He lived in a crude hut near the joiner's cottage and was always good with Mistress Skelton because she gave him food.

Now she beckoned him over, and Gowkie came and sat on his stool while she helped the boys remove their bundles and transfer them to Gowkie's back.

The minute they were free Robin and David shot off like arrows from a bow, David feeling very thankful that he was now strong enough to keep up with his friend.

Though they had been absent only a short time, the cottage seemed very quiet and forlorn, perhaps because the peat fire which usually burned day and night was just a heap of damp ashes. Mistress Skelton had taken care to pour plenty of water over it before she left—there was no need to help the raiders in their destructive work!

The boys went into the bedroom and Robin heaved David up on his shoulders to reach the little coffer down from the shelf. It wasn't very heavy but would be awkward to carry. They found an old cloak Mistress Skelton wore when she tended the pig and wrapping this round the coffer, made a long bundle they could carry between them.

As they retraced their steps, walking this time, the village appeared deserted, but the Abbey bell still tolled a slow, mournful chime.

Suddenly there was a strange screech behind them and a voice cried: 'Help! Oh, please help me!'

David was so startled he dropped his end of the bundle and swung round.

'Butter fingers!' snapped Robin, but he too turned to look. A thin, little girl with long, fair hair was coming towards them, a fat grey goose almost as big as herself struggling in her arms. The boys knew her well. She was the orphan grand-daughter of Widow Thwaite, a poor woman who made her living by nursing the sick. Their home was also at the far end of the village, near the joiner's.

'Why Margery, what are you doing?' asked Robin rather sharply; he was ashamed of being alarmed by a goose. 'Where's your grandmother?'

'She's gone to the Abbey—with the others—'panted the girl, 'But I had to catch Esmerelda—and she's already got away twice. Oh, do help. Please! OOOCH!'

The bird had wrenched one wing free and struck Margery such a blow on the face that she loosened her grip altogether. Esmerelda immediately flapped off in the direction the children had just come.

'Why on earth didn't you tie her feet?' demanded Robin.

'I—I don't know,' said Margery, 'I didn't think of it. Oh, do help me catch her.'

'Oh, leave her, and come with us,' Robin was growing impatient, 'the gates will shut any minute.'

'Oh no,' cried Margery, 'I can't do that. She's the most valuable thing we have.'

'I'll stay with Margery,' volunteered David, 'You go on.'

'No fear,' answered Robin, 'I'm not leaving you after last time! Mother would be furious. But what about this coffer?'

'We'll hide it,' said David, 'under that holly would be all right. The raiders would never look for it there and we can come back for it afterwards.'

The holly was a large bush forming part of a hedge round somebody's garden, and there was a pile of dead leaves under it. They tucked the coffer deep among them till it couldn't be seen.

'Now,' said Robin with satisfaction, 'let's catch this goose.'

But Esmerelda had no intention of being caught. Back and forwards she ran, trying always to reach one of the numerous ditches the villagers had cut to drain their low-lying fields.

'Oh dear,' gasped Margery at last, 'we'll NEVER catch her!'

'I know,' said David, 'I've an idea. You take your mother's cloak'—Robin still had this garment over his arm—'then when we drive her towards you, run and throw the cloak right over her.'

Once more he and Margery darted after the bird and carefully headed Esmerelda in Robin's direction. When he judged the moment right, Robin sprang forward, flinging the cloak in front of him. But Esmerelda swerved clear, Robin tripped over a stone and fell.

'I'll get her next time!' he cried as he

scrambled to his feet, and pursuing the goose as fast as he could, at last managed to entangle her in the cloak.

'Oh, you are clever!' The others came up and helped him unfold the struggling bird.

'We'll keep her like this, now we've got her,' said Robin, 'Lend me your knife, David. I must make a hole. Mother won't mind—it's her old cloak.' As he spoke he cut a hole for Esmerelda's head to stick through and tied the rest of the garment round her like a sack. The goose couldn't escape.

In the excitement of the chase, the children had forgotten all about the Scots, so they sat down for a few minutes to regain their breath.

'It's a silly name for a goose—Esmerelda,' said Robin presently. 'Why do you call her that?'

'It isn't silly! It's a lovely name,' retorted Margery, 'It's out of an old romance. That's a story, you know, about knights and ladies, and tournaments, and magicians, and all kinds of things.'

'Oh, I'd like stories like that,' said David, 'how did you hear them?'

'Well, come to our place sometime,' invited

Margery, 'both of you. When Grandmother was young she worked in a castle and learnt all these tales. She loves to tell them and she'd be so glad to do it for you—especially as you've been so kind.'

'Saints! The bell's stopped!' cried Robin. 'We're barred out! Let's get the coffer at once and make for the woods.'

Leaving Margery sitting by the edge of a ditch nursing Esmerelda, they went back among the houses and had almost reached the holly bush, when they heard angry shouts from the direction of the Abbey gate where most of the cottages were clustered, and the clattering of many horses' hooves.

The raid had really begun!

'They're HERE!' excitement overcame Robin's good sense. 'Oh, I wonder if it's Nebless Nick! Come on, we must see everything!' He was about to rush towards the fighting, but David caught his arm. 'You're not afraid, are you, David?'

'N-no, of course not.' David wasn't exactly sure. Would his kind master and the other men be hurt? 'But there's Margery. Shouldn't we stay with her?'

'Oh, I suppose so.' Robin let himself be

turned back. 'But I wish we could see what happens. I'd like to be a soldier some day.'

Margery was watching for them anxiously, traces of tears on her pale, grubby face.

'They've come, haven't they?' and without waiting for an answer, she went on, 'I've been thinking. We can't run far carrying Esmerelda, but if we put her in this ditch—tied up like she is—she'd be quite safe. Unless she shrieks of course—but maybe the Scots wouldn't know a tame goose from a wild one.'

Both boys agreed that this was a good idea, they gently lowered Esmerelda into the ditch. There wasn't much water and she lay trussed up on the soft mud, seemingly quite resigned to her fate.

Margery could hardly bear to leave her. 'Couldn't we all hide in the ditch?' she suggested, 'they wouldn't see us.'

But at that moment they heard a yell and saw two horsemen leaping over the fence of the nearest cottage. The raiders were already in the village searching for plunder.

'Come quick!' cried David. 'They'll find Esmerelda if we don't get away from here.'

Margery gave a little sob and one last look

at her pet. Then lifting her tattered skirt with one hand and clasping David's with the other, she ran as fast as the boys.

Though it made progress much slower, they tried to reach the distant woods by keeping among the patches of still unreclaimed shrubs and undergrowth instead of by the open fields or the usual tracks.

Presently they came to an open space where there was a little hovel made of branches and so roughly thatched with reeds it could barely keep out a shower. It was Gowkie Graeme's home and the queer things lying about it, old tools, broken pots, coloured stones from the shore, were the treasures he spent his days collecting.

The children had no time to look at them, for with a fierce shout the two raiders they'd seen before, came crashing through the bushes. Without hesitation the children dived for the hut. But it was too late. They'd been seen!

'Come oot, ye skulking English rats!' cried one Scot.

'Aye, come oot!' bawled the other, 'or we'll ride oor nags reet over your bit hoose.'

The children huddled together terrified.

Gowkie's shelter was so small they could hardly move in it, and very dark for Gowkie lived mostly out of doors. It was horrible to hear the horses trampling about and not know what the raiders were going to do next.

'What's going on here?' A new man seemed to have joined the others.

'Just a wee few English, Wattie man,' answered the one who'd spoken first. 'We'll soon ha' them oot,' and with that a lance was poked through Gowkie's brushwood wall. Margery screamed. It had just missed her!

'Stay there,' whispered Robin, pushing her flat on the ground, 'we'll go out.'

The boys crawled through the doorway and pulled themselves to their feet, narrowly escaping being stepped on by the horses as they did so.

The raiders were wild looking men with pointed steel helmets and their body armour was dented and rusty. But although one of them had a long scar down the side of his face, none appeared quite as nightmarish as Nebless Nick was supposed to be. Perhaps they don't kill children thought David.

The Scots gave a cheer as the boys came out of their hiding place but it instantly changed to a groan when they saw who their victims were.

'Why they're only bit laddies!' said one contemptuously.

'Is there ony mair on ye?' asked another.

'No,' lied Robin boldly.

'I'll mak sure,' said the first, and he began tearing the walls of the shelter apart with his lance. Margery crept out, covering her face with her hands.

'All that trouble for a few ragged bairns.' The raider stopped poking about. 'Weel, there's naught to lift here.'

'That yin's no so ragged,' said the second, 'he's got a braw tunic that would fit my ain laddie. Off wi' it noo!' He pointed his lance towards Robin's chest.

'T-take off my tunic?' gasped Robin.

'Aye, OFF!' shouted the raider, and swinging his lance round struck Robin a quick blow on the shins. 'Off, I say!'

Sometimes David had envied Robin his smart green tunic, but not now, as he watched the Scot make Robin undress and hand over all his good clothes.

Then the horrid Scots roared with laughter as Robin, cold and ashamed, ran back into the ruins of Gowkie's hut.

But David wasn't to be spared.

'Noo ye,' said the raider waving his lance in David's direction. 'Strip!'

I shouldn't have been jealous of Robin, he thought to himself as he slipped out of his own neat, grey garment. But if you've only had one new outfit in the whole of your life, it's hard to part with it. And how foolish he felt with nothing on. He was glad to run after Robin.

'The lassie next,' said the raider rolling up the boy's clothes and tying them to his saddle.

'Nay, leave her be,' ordered the one with the scar, 'her dress is more holes than cloth— but . . .' he looked thoughtfully at Margery, 'I wish ye'd had some bit ribbon I could take to my ain puir sick lassie. I promised her something from this raid, for she wept sore when we rode awa'.'

Margery had kept her head down while the boys were being humiliated, wondering if her turn would come next, but his words made her look up at the raider. The eyes in his scarred face seemed surprisingly kind.

'What—what's wrong with your daughter, sir?' she asked.

'She was hit in the leg by an English arrow as she fled up the brae wi' the rest o' our folk. Noo she sits a' day by the tower window looking at the green meads where she'll never play again.'

'Oh! I—I'm sorry, sir,' Margery faltered—then impulsively she put her hand inside the front of her dress and drew out a tiny silver cross she was wearing on a cord round her neck. 'Will—will you give her this? It—it belonged to my mother. It was a love gift from my father when they got married. It's all I have of my own, sir.' She began to cry. 'My parents are dead.'

The other raiders jostled nearer.

'Ye're in luck, Wattie. Let's ha' a keek at it, man!'

'Share and share alike, Wattie. What say, I toss ye for it?'

'Nay,' said the scarred raider, 'a love gift can't be sold or wagered lest it bring ill fortune. The Holy Virgin bless ye, little lass. My Kirsty will be rarely pleased to know there's some good English.—Awa wi' ye, lads!'

He wheeled his horse quickly and made off, the others following. Margery turned to join the boys, weeping quietly.

'What did you have to do that for?' demanded Robin. He and David were crouched among the debris, trying to wrap some of Gowkie's rags round themselves, but they had heard every word of the conversation. 'You needn't give anything to a dirty Scot.'

'They're still people,' Margery answered, 'just like us.'

David squeezed her hand. He too had been sorry for the raider's child—but Robin wouldn't understand.

After scrabbling through all Gowkie's rubbish, the boys at last found a couple of old tunics. They were far too large but better than nothing.

'What sights we are!' Robin peered down at himself in disgust. 'We'll never be able to go near the village like this. They'll make fun of us.'

'They won't feel like laughing at anything if the cattle have been stolen,' said Margery practically, 'Oh, I wonder if Esmerelda's all right. We'd better stay here till we're sure we're quite safe. The other Scots might be worse than those ones.'

So the children settled down in the hut for

what seemed like several long hours, and Margery told them all she could remember of her grandmother's stories over and over again.

At last when the sun was sinking towards the west like a great ball of fire, the Abbey bell pealed joyfully as a signal that the raiders were far enough away not to be likely to return.

The children ran and found Esmerelda still safe in the ditch, but so subdued by her experience she let Margery drive her quietly home.

Then the boys went on to collect the little coffer and it was safe also. So they carried it back to the joiner's house where everything was exactly as they'd left it, for the raiders had turned back before they reached that end of the village.

Mistress Skelton arrived a few minutes later, accompanied by Gowkie Graeme. She had been very anxious about the boys and was so thankful to find them safe she couldn't say much about the loss of their clothes.

She told them she'd seen Master Skelton but only in the distance, helping his friends repair the most urgent damage. The raiders had broken into many cottages and also got away with a great number of cattle.

'Now, the first thing we must do is get the fire lighted again,' said Mistress Skelton, 'and then after we've had a meal I'll try to fix up some of Robin's old things for you to wear.'

So the boys went for chips and shavings from the workshop floor and Mistress Skelton worked away with her flint and steel till the fire was kindled. Then the boys piled on some bigger logs and the blaze was just going nicely when Master Skelton returned.

He was tired out and in an extremely bad temper. Mistress Skelton poured him some of her best home-brewed burnet wine and while he was drinking it, the joiner told them what had happened.

Although the villagers had been having their military practice every week and should have known how to ambush and repulse a much larger force of invaders, somebody had spoilt things by firing off his arrows before the proper command was given.

As a result several men had been seriously wounded, including Master Skelton's best friend, Seth Wilson, and the raiders had got through to the cattle pastures unopposed. Nobody would admit it was their fault and all the villagers were blaming each other.

'But I'd wager it was that thick skulled toss-pot Flockmaster or his lubberly son. All this summer they've been trying to make trouble at the practices—and now Captain as good as said there was no discipline in my division—' the joiner broke off and looked sternly at Robin. 'Don't you ever forget, my son, that the very first thing a soldier has to learn is to obey. I should whip you both for worrying Mother so much—' he always called Mistress Skelton Mother to both the boys and David was growing to think of her as one—'but as you were looking after Margery I'll let you off this time.'

The boys climbed the ladder to their loft bedroom under the thatch very quietly. David was more miserable than he'd been since he left Flockmaster's. He had never seen pleasant, gentle-spoken Master Skelton in such a bad mood before—and to think he'd contributed to it—when all these months he'd been trying so very hard to show how grateful he was for his new home and work.

And was it really possible Flockmaster could have caused so much trouble just to spite Master Skelton? It hardly seemed likely—and yet he seemed to remember the head shepherd mentioning other mean little tricks he'd played on people, trifles which had appeared as cleverness when he'd boasted about them—and of course, Garath was bad enough to do anything . . .

Then there was poor Seth Wilson—that kind man who'd given David his treasured knife—taken now by the Scots along with his belt and tunic. Suppose Seth were to die and his jolly, little curly-headed babies were left without a father. Oh dear, would there never be an end to the trouble the raiders had caused?

The next thing that did happen was that the Lord Warden who lived in Carlisle Castle and guarded the English Border Marches for the King, sent his clerks round the country-side to find out exactly what had been stolen. When they came to the village the boys described their lost clothes and the clerks wrote it all down on their great parchments, so that the Lord Warden could ask payment for them next time he had a truce meeting with the Scottish nobleman who looked after the northern side of the Border.

Brother Dominic had accompanied the clerks on their rounds, scowling fiercely, so that people wouldn't dare to claim for anything they hadn't really lost, and soon a story was going about that Garath had persuaded some of his crowd to say he, too, had had a smart new outfit stolen. But at the last minute the others decided not to take part in the deception and had confessed to Brother Dominic who set Garath a really severe penance.

'And perhaps that'll teach him to behave,' said Master Skelton grimly, 'we've enough difficulties to cope with at present, without Garath adding to them.'

Three : The Black Shadow

During the weeks following the raid it was as if a shadow lay over the village. Master Skelton's prophecy that the people who had lost animals and other goods would have to wait a long time for their compensation was proving true. For the Lord Warden now said it would be many months before there would be another Border Meeting at which he could put forward their claim. The villagers were very angry, especially when some fresh cattle which the monks had promised should be brought up from their estates in the south, failed to come too.

Seth Wilson and the other wounded men were still very sick. Widow Thwaite sat up at night helping to nurse them, while Margery roamed about all day searching for herbs to make into poultices and medicines for the invalids, and still more to be dried and kept for use in the winter.

The quarrels about who had shot the

unlucky arrows went on and on, growing worse all the time, some people taking one side and some another. Many hot words were spoken at the ale-house till at length Master Skelton and a few of the more serious men wondered if it wouldn't be best to ask My Lord Abbot to hold an inquiry and put everyone on their oath to say exactly what they'd seen at the time of the raid.

'I'd do it quickly too, if I were you,' advised Mistress Skelton one day when her husband was talking it over with her, 'Or they'll soon be coming to blows among themselves and then more folk will be hurt. The devil *always* finds mischief for idle hands to do,' she added, looking approvingly at the boys who were sitting on the doorstep carefully peeling rushes, which she would later dip in fat to make rush-lights for the dark winter days.

'Well, I'll try to see what we can arrange tomorrow,' promised the joiner. But the following day something happened so strange and sad that all personal disagreements were quite forgotten.

Brother John disappeared!

His last visit to the village had been to see some of the wounded men. He had prayed for the sufferers, heard their confession, spoken kindly to their wives, patted all the little children on the head, then set out to walk back to the Abbey—and NOBODY had seen him since!

The next morning—David knew he'd remember it all his life—while the villagers were discussing the mystery and the monks planning to send out search parties, Gowkie Graeme came crying to the joiner's door with a pair of dirty, wet sandals in his hand.

Gowkie did not speak clearly at the best of times, and now he was so agitated it took them a long while to understand his story. He had been following his usual custom of beachcombing along the banks of the tidal river when he'd found the sandals laid neatly together just as if someone was coming back for them. Gowkie knew the monks wore such things and it gradually dawned on him that they might have belonged to Brother John. Gowkie was far too much in awe of the monks to speak to them himself, so he'd come to see if Master Skelton would tell him what to do.

The good joiner left his work at once, and took Gowkie along to the Abbey where they were shown right into the presence of My Lord Abbot himself. And Master Skelton had to help poor trembling, stuttering Gowkie to tell his tale all over again.

My Lord Abbot was very patient and heard them through to the end. Then he blessed them both and gave Gowkie a silver penny, which Gowkie put in his mouth to see what it tasted like.

As for Brother John, it looked, said My Lord Abbot sadly, as if he had been trying to cool his feet after the dusty walk and somehow been swept away, perhaps by the current.

Remembering his own experience on the marsh, David was sure that this was what had happened. Not that it made things any better. A solemn Requiem Mass was held in the Abbey church, all black draped for the occasion and, except for the wounded, the whole village was there and everyone was weeping bitterly.

Afterwards nobody had any enthusiasm for their normal work, especially David who fretted and grew so listless Master Skelton at length decided something must be done.

'Look here, boys,' he began one morning

as they were eating their breakfast of bread and cheese washed down by Mistress Skelton's mild home-brewed ale for the grown-ups and foaming beakers of new milk for the boys, 'this can't go on! You know we've work to do and more than enough of it since that raid. The amount of repairs I've been asked about will keep us busy for months, and I could use an extra pair of apprentices instead of losing those I've got. Why, my chisels are rusty from David crying over them, and whenever I need Robin I don't know whether to look for him this end of the village or the other.' He paused for a moment and continued very gravely. 'The holy father, God bless him, is dead and gone—they do say drowning is a pleasant death. Nothing can bring him back and likely he'll be in Paradise now, where we'll maybe see him again some day if we try to do the best we can with our lives—and remember, that's all anyone can do, from My Lord Abbot riding in state to London to help the King make our laws, to poor humble craftsmen like ourselves who can only show what they feel by the work of their hands.

'So now boys, I want you to take the whole

day off. Go out to the woods and get all your sorrowing done. You needn't come home till sunset, but Mother here,' he smiled at Mistress Skelton, 'wants some fire-wood, so bring back as much as you can, and tomorrow I'll expect you at the bench ready to put your hearts into your job.'

David was surprised to hear the joiner talk so seriously. Though Master Skelton was kind to everyone and always attended the church services, he sometimes spoke disrespectfully of the monks and made jokes about them. But David wondered if when he was so fussy about getting all the details of their work right, he was really thinking about that other Craftsman whom dear Brother John always assured David used to finish His woodwork perfectly.

David made a great effort to stop snivelling again. Master Skelton was right, of course—and a whole day's holiday *would* be a treat.

As they went through the village the boys saw Margery busy in one of the gardens, so they stopped to ask if she would come with them.

'I wish I could,' she said, 'but we don't need

any more herbs, so today I've promised to help old Master Wise make his garden tidy. The Scots trampled it till it looked like a ploughed field and he does so want to get it right before the winter rain makes the ground too heavy to work. Still,' she added with a smile, 'I'm to have six eggs when we're finished and that'll be nice,'

The cultivated ground on the landward side of the Abbey was still surrounded by dense forest, and the boys made their way towards it, at first walking slowly and thoughtfully, till the loveliness of the mellow autumn day began to cheer them up.

The woods were beautiful. The sunlight glinted through the leaves of the great trees in ever changing shades of gold and green. Spider webs decorated with dew-drops hung like silver lace from the bushes. A few late birds sang sweetly and there were rabbits and squirrels everywhere. Once they thought they saw a deer whisking past in the undergrowth.

The boys knew better than to touch the crimson toadstools growing in the moss at their feet, but they hunted for the first hazel nuts and ate juicy black brambles till their hands and mouths were stained dark purple.

In the middle of the day they lay down in a little sunny glade and slept so soundly a butterfly alighting on Robin's nose made him wake up sneezing and accusing David of having tickled him.

After this they wandered on again, exploring further into the forest and enjoying themselves so much they nearly forgot they'd promised to bring back kindling for Mistress Skelton.

At last they unwillingly turned in the direction of home and began collecting all the fallen branches they could find. Soon, absorbed in their task, they moved further and further apart.

It was then that David came to a grassy clearing by the side of a small stream and stopped to arrange his load into a more convenient bundle. Just as he was doing this someone called his name—and it wasn't Robin's voice!

David dropped his sticks and looked about him in bewilderment.

'David! David!' came the voice again, and on the other side of the stream he saw a white figure standing among the bushes.

David stared hard at it and crossed himself. Mother of God, could he be having a vision! The figure was surely that of Brother John!

'It's all right, David. I'm not a spirit,' came Brother John's usual gentle voice.

'Oh, father! we thought . . . '

'You thought I was drowned, didn't you? And that was just what you were supposed to think—Stop!' he added sharply as David was about to wade across the stream. 'Don't come a step nearer, David! But tell me, are you alone? I've been praying for someone trustworthy to come along.'

'No, father. Robin's here.' David was puzzled by Brother John's behaviour.

'Ah, yes. Robin, of course. Well, fetch him and I'll talk to you both together.'

Robin had already heard their voices and was coming towards them, peering cautiously round the trees to see who David was talking to. But when David turned to bring him nearer he fled in fright.

'Don't be silly, Robin! It's Brother John! He's alive and safe!' cried David racing after him, and Robin nervously allowed himself to be led back to the clearing.

'Sit by that tree, the one with the ivy on it,'

the monk told them, making his voice very distinct so that they could hear clearly across the space. 'You remember that afternoon I er—disappeared, and you'll have heard—the village being what it is—that I was visiting poor Seth Wilson and the others—you must tell me how they are before we part. But back to my story. After I'd left them I thought I'd just walk along by the lower infield, to the place the men fenced off last week and see how many sheep they'd put to graze on the stubble there. As I reached it, I saw a man staggering about on the track beyond as if he were the worse for liquor. I went towards him and he fell to the ground, and then I realized he wasn't drunk but ill. For when he saw a priest bending over him, he said: 'Hear my sins, father—I've caught the plague as a punishment for them.'

The boys were sitting as enthralled as when Brother John told them scripture tales.

'Did he die, father?' asked David as the monk paused.

'No, he's here,' Brother John pointed to the bushes behind him, 'lying on a bed of dry bracken in a little shelter I made. You see I couldn't take him to the village. There's been too much trouble lately. If they thought the plague had come as well, there would be a panic and no more work done before winter. My brethren at the Abbey also have enough to worry about at present—so we're just staying here,' he smiled ruefully and went on. 'Actually I'm not sure my patient has the plague—there are no reports of it being near—but he believes he has it and imagined illnesses can be quite as bad as real ones, you know.

'Fortunately the weather is warm now, so we're taking no harm. The difficulty is food. I find I'm not as good at setting snares as when I was young. But could you bring something to eat? I'm not asking you to steal—though that would be permissible under the circumstances—but Mistress Skelton keeps a good table and I'm sure she could spare us something.'

'Oh, she'd be pleased to,' cried Robin, 'and she won't tell anyone.'

'No,' said Brother John firmly, 'she mightn't mean to, but when people are worried and frightened they let things slip out. The plague is a very terrifying and serious illness, my children. If you can just bring a little food yourselves we'll do well enough.'

'I'll give you mine,' said David quickly, 'I'm used to not eating much—and Robin can bring it. His father will only think he's off playing again.'

'Then put it in the hollow under the roots of that tree you're sitting by and I'll collect it when you've gone.'

'Couldn't we tell Margery?' asked Robin, 'she's often in the woods gathering herbs for her grandmother.'

'Margery?' Brother John considered. 'Ah, yes. The girl who shared your encounter with the Scots. You had some teasing about that didn't you? Yes, she's a sensible little maid. Widow Thwaite has taught her to keep quiet about other people's affairs. You may tell Margery, but no one else, remember. We can't take risks.'

The two boys said goodbye to the monk, shouldered their faggots and set off for home, wondering what would be for supper and if they could get any of it.

A very savoury smell met them as they entered the kitchen.

'There you are,' Mistress Skelton greeted them, 'I've a good pan of broth waiting for you. Why, what's the matter?' The boys were looking at each other in dismay. Broth couldn't be carried without a dish. 'Aren't you hungry?'

'Oh yes,' cried Robin. After their long day in the open air they certainly were.

David managed to conceal a piece of bread while Robin described all their adventures—except the most important one!—to his parents. Then David had an idea.

'Margery has eggs,' he whispered as they rose from their stools.

Robin nodded his understanding, and turning to his mother told how they had seen Margery working hard and asked if he could take her a faggot.

'Yes, do,' Mistress Skelton looked pleased. It was seldom Robin thought of doing things for anyone else. 'Take a nice big one.'

Margery was thrilled when she heard what had happened.

'Oh, how WONDERFUL!' she exclaimed, clapping her hands. 'Why, he's just like the saints! Oh, I do wish I'd been with you! I know that clearing well.'

'You'll help us get them some food?' urged Robin, 'Your eggs?'

Margery's face clouded over. 'I'd have loved to give you them. Oh, I would, I would! But I can't. When I was going home Garath knocked me down and they all smashed. Look . . . ' she showed them a yellow daub on the front of her dress and a tear in the skirt which revealed a sorely scratched knee. 'Grandmother's going to wash and patch it when she comes home.'

'The spiteful dastard!' swore Robin.

David merely clenched his fists and wished—not for the first time—that he was big and strong enough to fight Garath. There was nothing they could do but return home where Robin indignantly recounted what had happened.

'Just like Garath!' commented Mistress Skelton, but her husband was furious and with a muttered oath went out into the evening twilight. Master Skelton shared something of Robin's impulsiveness.

'I doubt if Flockmaster's family have a laying hen let alone eggs,' said Mistress Skelton, 'but if anything can be done your father will do it.'

She was right. The joiner came back grinning broadly.

'Gave Garath the thrashing of his life!' he announced, 'and he's sent this for Margery.' Triumphantly he held out a farthing. But the boys exchanged disappointed looks. Money was all right but you couldn't eat it.

'Margery will be pleased,' said Mistress Skelton as she hustled them off to bed, 'you can take it to her before work in the morning.'

To their surprise Margery met them with a radiant smile.

'I'm rich!' she cried. 'Do you know what happened! Old master Wise saw Garath knock me down and though he'd no more eggs himself, he told his neighbours and they each gave me one. I've got ten now! Grandmother's been out all night so she doesn't know yet. I'll leave her five and take the rest to Brother John right away.'

They gave Margery the farthing which she said she'd put aside for her grandmother, and a piece of cheese David had saved from his breakfast. Carrying this and the eggs, Margery ran off as lightly as a fawn.

For a week she went back and forwards taking such scraps of food as they could obtain without being noticed. While the boys stuck to their work so well Master Skelton was delighted and said they could have another ramble in the woods to collect firing. So next day found all three of them seated by the hollow tree. They whistled and Brother John appeared on the opposite side of the stream. His thin face looked more lined than ever, but he smiled warmly.

'I've been thinking it's hardly right allowing you to keep pilfering food for me—and my patient is worse. I must have more help. I'm grateful for your herbs, little Margery, but possibly some of the medications Brother Infirmarian gets from foreign parts might suit him better. So I want you to do something else for me. I want you to go and tell Brother Dominic where I am and ask him to come here.'

The children looked at each other doubtfully. Finding and bringing food had been rather fun—but to talk to Brother Dominic!

'Don't look so surprised,' the monk continued. 'Brother Dominic and I are very good friends—although we don't always see eye to eye, and my dear brother often forgets the pranks we used to play when *we* were young. For we were brought up in the same village, you know, far away from here.'

'When must we tell him?' asked Margery.

'Tonight, after service, go to the alms gate and ask whoever's in charge if you can see Brother Dominic. I wish I'd writing materials but I haven't, so you must be careful. Say I beg him to come here by the memory of our pilgrimage to the shrine of St Ninian at Whithorn—it was as the result of that pilgrimage we decided to enter the religious life. Now, can you remember those words? Let me hear you repeat them.'

'Where is Whithorn?' asked Margery curiously, when they'd said them over and over again.

'In the south-west of Scotland on the other side of the Solway Firth,' Brother John told her. 'There's a beautiful white church there where Blessed St Ninian who brought the light of Christianity to our land, used to preach.'

'I'm not carrying any messages to Brother Dominic,' said Robin as the children made their way homeward.

'I don't want to either,' confessed Margery, 'he always glares worse at me than at anyone else. You'll have to do it, David. The monks like you.'

David hardly agreed with her, but he nodded gloomily. Somebody had to help Brother John. At supper he was so pale and ate so little Mistress Skelton imagined he must be sickening for something.

'If you don't look better by bedtime I'll have to prepare a herbal draught for you,' she said as the boys went out for what she supposed would be a last game before dark.

'Shall we come as far as the gate with you?' asked Robin as David was about to set off.

'No,' David said shortly. He was terrified, his hands were cold and clammy, and his stomach turning over. But he realized it was his own ordeal, and having the others beside him like a bodyguard wasn't going to make one bit of difference to the way he felt inside. They were only going to wait at the gate. Even the best of friends can't share somebody else's fear.

His heart thumped loudly as he neared the monastery. It was far worse than facing the Scots, because then everything had happened so quickly that he'd been too excited to be really frightened.

But this, this was nearly as bad as when Brother Dominic sent him back to the marsh to find the lost sheep. Though now, he tried to keep reminding himself, he wasn't a pitiful little waif any more. He was Master Skelton's young apprentice, and becoming more one of the family every day. Besides he knew, deep down in his mind—and would never have mentioned it to anyone—that although he was just learning how to handle his tools, he would in the finish, be a far, far better craftsman than slapdash Robin.

However none of these encouraging thoughts helped much and he felt very small indeed as he mingled with the oldest and poorest of the village who were waiting at the alms gate. Among them he saw Gowkie Graeme and a few wandering beggars who'd come to see if they could share the evening dole of bread and cabbage soup.

David joined the queue and on reaching the monk in charge of the distribution, asked to speak to Brother Dominic.

'You want to see Brother Dominic?' the man echoed. 'Are you sure you mean Brother Dominic?'

'Yes,' said David, hardly recognizing his

own voice.

The monk turned and repeated the message to someone inside, then with a sort of you're-for-it-now look, bade David stand apart and wait.

When the tall, dark monk appeared David's knees knocked.

'You have a message for me, boy? Repeat it!'

Why couldn't Brother Dominic remember anyone's name? David trembled still more. It was just like being a beetle waiting to be crushed under Brother Dominic's feet.

'Y-yes, I-I've a message father. It-it's from Brother John.' David knew he was stuttering worse than Gowkie Graeme, but he couldn't help it.

Brother Dominic's face turned purple and his voice thundered. 'From Brother John! You blasphemous young cur! How dare you come here with such a tale! Our saintly brother was drowned and is in the abode of bliss.'

'But-but he's not,' stammered David, 'he's in the w-woods and he asks you to come to him for the sake of your visit . . .' would he get it out right? 'your pilgrimage to the-the shrine of the Blessed Saint-Saint Ninian at Whithorn.'

'Holy Mary and All the Saints! WHAT are you saying?'

The next minute Brother Dominic was down on his haunches with an arm round David's shoulders and his face on a level with the boy's.

'So it's David—David the miracle worker! What was it you said then? Now, take your time and tell me everything slowly.' So David told him.

'We must go at once!' Brother Dominic straightened himself, 'Nay, it is too near dusk—even with a lantern it would be difficult to find the way. At first light then. Tell Master Skelton I have an urgent task for you.'

The joiner was amused when he heard this.

'I hope I'm not going to lose my apprentice to the cloister,' he joked.

Early as it was when they set off, David knew other eyes than Robin's and Margery's were watching them. Everybody would be wondering where he was going with such an unlikely companion and he hoped they wouldn't think he was getting above himself again.

Brother Dominic was his usual forbidding self so David kept quiet till they reached the clearing where he gave the usual whistle with great vigour. In a few minutes Brother John came out of the undergrowth. At the sight of him Brother Dominic would have leaped across the stream, but David grasped his habit and tried to hold him back.

Brother John burst out laughing. 'Oh David, you just look like a herd holding a refractory bullock by its tail! Be calm, Dominic, my dearest brother, I beg you, and listen to what I've to say.'

They talked together for a long while. But David couldn't understand much of the conversation because it was mostly Latin and long words. So he just sat watching them, wondering how many years it took to become a scholar, and thinking how much nicer Brother Dominic looked when he smiled instead of frowning. He was actually quite handsome.

David came out of his day-dream to find they were talking about him.

'We are forgetting David . . .'

'The boy should be back at his work.'

'Yes; but David,' Brother John smiled mischievously, 'tell Master Skelton that Brother Dominic says you have done his errand so well you are to have another half holiday in the woods on Saturday.'

'Oh, thank you, father!' David exclaimed, 'May Robin come too?'

'Yes, of course. And Margery also if her grandmother can spare her.'

Master Skelton raised his eyebrows in mock horror when David gave him the message. 'By Our Lady, you'll have to watch out, David. They'll be making a monk of you yet.'

It was a dull misty day when they returned to the clearing. Autumn had really come at last. The bright leaves were falling limply from the damp trees, the moss was soggy underfoot, and the birds and animals seemed to have hidden themselves away.

The news was both good and bad. Brother Infirmarian's physic had made the invalid take a rapid turn for the better and Brother John's wise advice had brought him to a more sensible frame of mind. That evening he was to be carried to the sickroom at the Abbey where he could finish his convales-

cence in comfort.

'And then,' said Brother John, who being now quite sure his patient hadn't had the plague after all, was sitting at the foot of the oak tree with his arms round the children, 'I am to go to our other monastery at Melrose in Scotland for a rest and change of air, till such time as My Lord Abbot thinks fit to explain my disappearance to the village.'

'Don't be frightened,' he went on quickly, for at the mention of Scotland, David had clutched at his hand with a terrified grasp. 'I'll be quite safe you know, the Scots don't harm priests. We can go freely from one monastery to another in all countries—and Melrose is only a few days' journey away. God willing I'll be back by Christmas or maybe even sooner. So don't look so doleful, my children.'

Everything happened just as Brother John said. At the feast of All Saints a service of great rejoicing was held at the Abbey and My Lord Abbot, wearing his most gorgeous vestments of purple and gold and glittering with jewels, offered prayers of thanksgiving for the good monk's prompt and heroic action which had saved the village from a plague scare.

Meantime the sick stranger had quietly gone away when he was strong enough to travel and nobody expected to hear any more about him.

But one day a packman came to the village, dropped a gold coin in the alms dish at the church and then asked his way to the joiner's. He was a friend of the former invalid and had promised to bring gifts for all the children. A plain blue dress for Margery—the first new one she'd ever had—and two smart tunics with bright red leather belts for the boys.

'Oh—ho! Just wait till Garath sees these!' Robin was peering at himself in the small piece of polished steel which served his mother as a hand mirror. 'When can we go out in them?'

'Not till Easter,' said Mistress Skelton firmly, 'they must be kept fresh for the holy festival. No one wears their new clothes before then. And you needn't grumble,' she went on, seeing a rebellious look on Robin's face. 'Widow Thwaite isn't going to allow Margery to wear hers either. Nor must you go boasting about them to the other boys. We've had quite enough jealousy and bad feeling in the village. Flockmaster's still got a grudge against your father—and that thrashing he gave Garath didn't help—though Garath deserved it if ever a boy did! But it looks like being a trying winter and they could succeed in making trouble before it's over.'

'Garath did look sorry for himself the day after Father hit him,' said Robin with a grin. 'All right, Mother. We won't talk about our good luck.'

Four : The Stormy Spring

Brother John's return and their new clothes were the last nice things to happen for a long time. The winter began early and was exceptionally cold. The distant mountains, usually so blue and friendly, were peaked with white, and though snow did not lie long in the cultivated place beside the warm western sea, the ground remained frozen iron-hard for months.

One of the wounded men died, but the others gradually recovered. Seth Wilson was among them and on fine days, if the paths were not too slippery with ice, he would hobble about the village on a crutch Master Skelton had made him.

The rest of the villagers, bored and frustrated at not being able to get on with their work on the land, just stood around grumbling, and Flockmaster's rough voice was loudest among them.

At last My Lord Abbot thought they'd

been idle long enough and needed some exercise, so he sent along a large wooden top which the men were supposed to whip from one end of the village to the other. Sometimes the monks joined in the game and it was fun to see Brother John and Brother Dominic hitching up their habits and trying to see who could send the top whirling farthest.

But food had been scarce ever since the raid and many of the people were so miserable they couldn't be amused by anything. Even the joiner's household was not as cheerful as usual. The workshop was so chilly, their hands grew numb and chilblains made it painful to handle their tools, and fewer jobs were brought in because nobody had the means of paying.

The only corn Mistress Skelton could buy from the Abbey mill was poor stuff which normally would have been given to the horses. Her good broth also became more watery as time went on, but thanks to the way she'd looked after David during the summer, and the new warm working tunic she'd made him from the one Robin had outgrown, he didn't suffer too much. Nor did Robin; but Margery became thinner than ever and her blue eyes seemed enormous in her peaked face. There were no gardening jobs and no herbs to gather now, and though her grandmother still helped with the sick she did it for kindness only. And every day they stood with the other helpless ones at the alms gate just to get enough food to keep them alive.

During really bad weather Widow Thwaite tried to teach her to spin, but Margery hated sitting still and whenever there was a little sunshine she drove Esmerelda out to the common land to find some grass that wasn't too frozen for the goose to eat.

At midwinter the great church glittered with candles as once more the singing of the Christ Mass rose to the rafters, but there was no feasting, no roast ox, and no merriment in the hearts of the villagers.

A few days after the Christmas feast—or Christmas fast—as Master Skelton gloomily called it—ploughing should have started but the ground was still unworkable.

As soon as it was dark people went to bed. Candles and rushlights were scarce, and in any case their light was so feeble you couldn't do much by it.

One night, when Robin as usual had

dropped off first, David was lying watching the moonlight shine through the chinks in the window shutter, and thinking of all kinds of things, especially the lessons he'd just learnt.

For even when there wasn't much work Master Skelton still remembered he was trying to train good craftsmen, and getting the boys together would make them repeat all about the different kinds of wood, what each was best suited for, and the correct joints for particular tasks. Then afterwards, if they did well, he would tell them how, when he was young, he'd travelled to the south of England and over to the Continent, visiting famous churches and studying the beautiful wood-carvings in them.

Suddenly David heard a sound, a most unusual sound just outside the cottage. It was like somebody crying. He listened for a minute or two. Could it be someone in trouble—or a rogue trying to trick them into opening the door? He wondered if he should go for his master but decided to wake Robin first.

'Oh, go away, David,' muttered Robin as David shook him. 'What do you want?'

'Listen, there's somebody outside,' whispered David. 'I don't know what to do, and I can't move the bolt anyway.'

Robin sat up, all thought of sleep gone. 'It's somebody calling our names. It's like a girl. Let's go down and see.'

He was right. When they'd groped their way down the loft ladder it was easy to recognize Margery's voice. Robin drew back the heavy wooden bar securing the door and opened it.

'Oh, thanks be to Our Lady! I thought I'd never make you hear! I'm in such trouble! Garath's stolen Esmerelda!' Margery gave a sob. 'Grandmother is spending the night with Mistress Penryse who has a new baby, and I was all alone when I heard noises. So I peered out and there was Garath—I saw him as plain as anything—going off with Esmerelda. Oh, do help me get her back before he kills her.'

Hastily the boys put on their shoes and the three children raced through the village. The moon was right overhead making it as light as day.

'He's been wanting her for a long time,' panted Margery, 'when I was going to the common—he threatened to take her. He used to say—people like us—shouldn't have fat geese—when their neighbours were starving.'

'Bah! They've geese of their own,' said Robin, 'and poor scraggy things they are too—not like Esmerelda.'

'Of course not! *We* share all we have with Esmerelda.'

Flockmaster's cottage, well away from the rest of the houses, on the path to the marsh, was an untidy place without a neat garden such as the other villagers took pride in. Instead it was surrounded by stinking manure heaps, filthy pig-sties, and numerous pens where the sheep could be kept for shearing. David knew his way among them only too well.

'The geese are over here,' he said, leading the way to a pen near the cottage. 'But how'll we know which is Esmerelda?'

'She'll come to me,' said Margery confidently and, slipping into the enclosure, she held out her hand calling softly: 'Essie! Essie! Come here. Good goosie. Come on, Es.'

Immediately one of the birds left the rest and waddled towards them. 'Catch her quick!' cried Margery, and Robin sprang at the goose, pinioning her with his strong arms, while David stood ready to close the gate.

But Esmerelda didn't appreciate being rescued so roughly. Her shriek rang through the night stillness and set all the other geese trumpeting in chorus.

'Oh, Holy Virgin! They'll wake everybody!' gasped Margery, 'Oh, Robin, don't let go of her. Oh, Saints protect us! Here's Garath!'

The big lad had come to the door and was looking about him.

'Crouch down,' whispered David. 'Perhaps he won't see us.'

They squatted by the side of the pen, Robin nearly choking Esmerelda in an effort to keep her quiet. But Garath must have guessed what was happening for he came striding straight towards them.

'Oh, he's coming,' Margery was terrified, 'and he's got a big stick!'

Robin raised his head to look and for a second loosed his hold of Esmerelda. She broke free from him and flapped right across Garath's path. Lifting his stick, the youth turned after her but with a scream Margery darted forward, getting between him and the goose. At the same instant the boys charged. David sprang for Garath's right arm and

Robin gave him a kick on the leg which made him stumble. Then while he was off balance they gave him a hard push—right into the nearest manure heap!

Leaving him floundering in the foul mess the children ran on, but Garath's curses as he struggled to rise, brought a new danger. Glancing back they saw Flockmaster's burly figure emerging from the cottage followed by all Garath's brothers and sisters, running to see what was happening. At the same time Flockmaster shouted an order and two black and white shapes sprang barking into the moonlight.

'He's setting the dogs on us!' wailed Margery, 'We can't escape!'

'It's all right. Run quick!' cried David, 'I'll send them back.'

Robin and Margery fled, with Esmerelda waddling hurriedly before them, determined to be safe in her own home.

The dogs knew David for he'd often lain cuddled up for warmth beside them on the floor. Now they danced round him, licking his face with wet, friendly tongues. David hugged them in turn and stroked their shaggy heads.

'There, good dogs! Nice old Meg! Kind Lassie! Go home now! HOME, good dogs!' Obediently they trotted off. But David had been recognized.

'It's that young rascal David,' bawled Flockmaster, 'bringing his mates to steal our geese!'

With a sinking heart David tore after the others, but didn't say anything till they'd parted from Margery and were back in bed once more.

'Oh, stop worrying. Father will believe our story,' was all Robin's response. 'But don't let's talk about it till we see what happens. Holy Mary, I'm tired! We must get some sleep.'

He turned round and drew the covers over his head.

Nothing was said the next day or the day after, and as time went on the children decided Flockmaster and Garath must have realized they were in the wrong and decided to keep quiet.

The frost had now given way to soft wet weather, and the patches of white in the gardens were snowdrops instead of heaps of hailstones from the last cold shower. Long brown lamb's tails dangled from the hazel trees and the willow shoots were tipped with silver as the catkins began to burst forth in readiness for Palm Sunday.

But first came Shrove Tuesday celebrations, the last chance of merry-making before the six weeks of Lent. It was, of course, a holiday, so in the afternoon Robin went to watch a cock-fight at the ale-house. David and Margery, who didn't like seeing things hurt, wandered off to the fields to see if they could find enough nettles and other plants for both Mistress Skelton and Widow Thwaite to make herb puddings.

When they came back Robin was looking very glum. He'd wagered all his money, two farthings, on a cock which had been defeated, and he scowled when his father said: 'Cheer up! If you will gamble you must expect to lose oftener than you win.'

It surprised David to see Robin so depressed, for during the days that followed he scarcely ever mentioned the cock-fight. Though everyone else was saying it had been the most exciting for many years, and however had the owners managed to keep the birds in such good condition through the hard winter.

Another strange thing was that Robin hardly went out any more, and stuck to his work as if he couldn't bear to waste a minute. Nor did he tease and chatter as he generally did. David was very worried. Surely losing two farthings couldn't be so dreadful. As his father had said, Robin knew the risk. Perhaps he'd been wanting to buy something special. But if so, why couldn't they earn some more money? Do a job for someone? He, David, would gladly help.

One morning when they were alone in the workshop, David could stand the silence no longer.

'Did you mind losing your farthings very much, Robin?' he asked.

'Farthings?' said Robin, 'What are you talking about? Oh, at the cock-fight.—Of course not.'

'Then what's the matter?' persisted David, 'I know something's bothering you.'

To his amazement Robin threw down his tools and burst out passionately: 'Oh David, you're right! I don't know what to do. They're saying such awful things . . . '

'They? Who?'

'Flockmaster and Garath—at the cock-fight. They'd been drinking, and they said Father was a HERETIC!'

'A HERETIC!' David crossed himself.

'Yes. But he couldn't be—not Father. Oh David, I'm so worried. I—I don't know what to do. I—I think they burn heretics. And there's Mother as well. I can't talk to anyone about it. Oh David, you're much braver than I am, and clever too, although you're so small. What do you think I should do?'

But David had no answer to this.

As the evenings were now so light, the children always went out for a game before bedtime. That night they were not in a mood for play but trailed aimlessly about till Margery came up and said her grandmother was wanting to speak to them.

Rather surprised, they followed her to her home where Widow Thwaite, a tall thin old woman was sitting on a stool by the peat fire in the middle of the room. She was busy spinning wool from a distaff and as she talked her long, brown fingers never ceased moving.

'It's you I want, young Master Skelton,' she began, fixing her eyes on Robin. 'You've been good to my Margery—and that goose of hers—' with a smile she looked towards a dark corner where Esmerelda was sitting quietly in a basket. 'Your parents are kind too, always ready to help those not so well off as themselves.' She paused for a moment. 'I hear a lot when I go about people's houses—and I don't generally repeat it—but this time I will. Your father can read, can't he?' she asked abruptly.

'Why, yes. I believe he can.' Robin was rather taken aback. He'd never seen his father practise this unusual skill, but now he remembered that when Master Skelton described the famous churches he'd visited he'd talked about reading texts painted on the walls—so—he must be able to read.

'Well, there's some in this village jealous of him for that and other things—and jealousy makes folk spiteful and cruel. Your father'll be away next week, won't he?'

'Oh yes,' Robin was sure of his facts this time, 'he's going down south to choose timber for some new panelling in the Abbey guest house.'

Widow Thwaite nodded. 'Yes, that's it. That's what they don't like. They think he's getting too much favour from those over there,' she jerked her head in the direction of the monastery, 'and sometimes Master Skelton speaks his mind a bit more freely than is wise. But listen to what I've to say—and not a word outside these walls. Mind that, you David.'

David stiffened. 'Of course not!' He might be poor but he wasn't disloyal. How dare she!

Widow Thwaite was going on: 'Flockmaster and a few who have a spite at Master Skelton say he has a parchment which ordinary folk aren't supposed to read. So while he's away they mean to come to your house and find it. Then they'll take it to the Abbey and Master Skelton will be in serious trouble.'

'What's the parchment about?' asked Robin bewildered, 'Witchcraft?'

'Oh, bless you, no!' the old woman seemed grimly amused, 'It's supposed to be the scriptures translated into English by some foolish heretics who imagine they know more about God's Word than the Lord Abbot or our Holy Father the Pope in Rome—but never mind all that. Just tell your father to get rid of that parchment quickly. For as soon as his

back's turned they'll be along looking for it, sure as I'm sitting here! If I get to know when they're coming I'll send warning, but we'll have to be careful. *I* don't want trouble either. So off you go and remember what I've told you. And now, Margery child, what about going on with your work.'

Giving her friends an anxious little smile, Margery quickly took up two pieces of wood set with sharp metal teeth and began teasing out more wool for her grandmother to spin.

As the boys ran home in the sweet spring dusk, a man with the Holm Cultram coat of arms on his jacket was just coming away from the joiner's house. It was one of the Abbey servants who had brought a message to say that the party for the south were leaving earlier than expected. News had come about a band of robbers, made desperate by the bad winter, who were planning to attack the convoy, and so by setting off the next day it was hoped to avoid them.

Indoors there was no time for talk. Mistress Skelton bustled around getting out her husband's best clothes and packing food for the journey, while Master Skelton was finishing urgent jobs in the workshop and giving the boys last minute instructions at the same time.

The following morning they got up before dawn and went to see the long train of pack-horses, wagons, servants, and men-at-arms leaving the Abbey, with Master Skelton riding beside them on a borrowed horse.

He would be returning in about two weeks but as it was the first time he'd been away since they were married, Mistress Skelton was a bit anxious.

The boys decided not to add to her worry by mentioning the parchment, but in the next few days they couldn't help noticing some of the villagers giving them queer looks and most of their play-fellows seemed to be avoiding them.

One afternoon they were mending the garden fence which had been broken by a herd of cattle rushing past on their way to fresh pasture, when Margery came skipping along.

'Can't stop!' she cried, swinging the rope over her head, and hissed under her breath, 'Grandmother says tomorrow!'

'Well, we'll have to tell Mother now, I suppose,' said Robin.

Mistress Skelton was sceptical when she heard their story. 'So that's what Widow Thwaite was hinting at the other day. I couldn't make her out, and I'm sure there's no parchment or anything like that here. At least he's never said anything about one. But we can look and see. It isn't in the chest or the little coffer and it certainly isn't in the spice cupboard by the fire.'

They searched the kitchen, the bedroom, the boys' attic and the workshop without any luck.

'Perhaps he gave it away,' said Mistress Skelton hopefully, 'or maybe folk are just imagining things. We'll see what tomorrow brings.'

The next day was so calm and sunny it seemed impossible for anything unpleasant to happen, but sure enough, towards noon, Flockmaster, Garath and the rest appeared making their way towards the joiner's cottage.

'Oh, here they are!' cried Robin who had been running back and forwards to the gate all the morning. 'Now, let's bar the door and keep them out.'

'No, they'd only break it down,' answered his mother. 'Be quiet and let me talk to them.'

She shooed the boys into the house and waited for the men to come up the garden path.

'What do you want, good people?' Mistress Skelton asked calmly. 'My husband's away as you know, and any business you have with him will have to await his return.'

'We want that sinful parchment he has—not fit for Christians, it isn't. We'll show it to Brother Dominic. Just wait till the holy fathers know what you are. Heretics every one!' stormed Flockmaster. 'And I'll have my herd boy back that you stole too.'

David clutched Robin's arm. He was beginning to feel frightened, but Mistress Skelton was speaking again.

'This is nonsense,' she said loudly and clearly, 'and you know it, neighbours. My husband's as good a Christian as any of you. Who's ever heard of him missing Mass or Confession? And if you've anything against him, why can't you tell him to his face? The monks gave David into our care because he was being ill treated. And as for having a forbidden writing, I tell you we haven't and wouldn't have. But—' the men were getting restless, they had been at the ale-house—

104

'come in and see for yourselves. Now, where would we keep such a thing?' She scornfully indicated the bare kitchen with the bedroom opening off it, and the simple wooden furniture made by the joiner himself.

But the men pushed rudely past her and began poking about all over the little home. One of them rummaged through the great clothes chest, dragging out Mistress Skelton's best dress and crumpling it. Another tore off the bed-covers, and David was sure by the expression on Garath's face that when he knocked the best cooking pot from the shelf it was done deliberately.

Mistress Skelton apparently thought so too, for she closed the lid of the big chest very sharply and sat down on it, drawing Robin near to her, as if afraid his hot temper might lead to some rash action.

'I wonder what *your* wife would say if you did this at home?' she remarked to one of the men. He looked rather ashamed.

'I think we owe you an apology, mistress,' he replied, 'Come on, lads, let's leave them in peace. We'll not find anything.'

'What, you're not giving up yet, are you?' cried Garath. 'I'll find that thing if I've to tear the place apart.'

The men had already been round the workshop, but now Garath ran back there, brought out a ladder, and setting it against the house, began to pull off the thatch by the armful.

'Oh, do stop him,' begged Mistress Skelton, 'we'll have no roof left.'

But as she spoke Garath gave a triumphant shout.

'Got it! I told you so! Look here—' he descended the ladder holding a long round leather case. 'Now, let's open it. Ho! Ho! Wait till Brother Dominic sees this!'

He took off one end of the case and drew out a roll of parchment which he unfolded.

'What is it? Let's see.' The men pressed round very curious. For most of them it was the first time they'd ever seen writing and the heavy black lettering was a complete mystery to them. Garath couldn't read either and he wasn't really interested. Having found it and the prospect of doing the joiner a bad turn was all that mattered.

So when a man called from within the cottage, 'I've found something too! Look at this!' Garath hurried to join another group who had got the little coffer down from the shelf and were eagerly counting the money in it.

'Come on, let's have some for our trouble,' said Flockmaster, and they began sharing out the coins among themselves.

'You wicked thieves!' Robin was unable to contain himself any longer. 'That's my father's money!'

'He'll not need it when the good Lord Abbot's seen that paper. Heretics can't own anything. Come on, Garath, let's take it to the Abbey.'

Garath looked about him. In the excitement he'd forgotten the parchment. 'I—I put it down,' he muttered, going outside and staring round rather stupidly. 'I left it on the wall.'

They all rushed to the low stone wall between the garden and the pig sty.

'Maybe the sow's eaten it,' suggested someone, as they hunted among the plants on one side of the wall and the pig's sludge on the other.

'If it was evil, Garath, the devil's maybe gone with it!' cried one timid fellow. The others took up the idea.

'Come on, let's get away! There's magic here!'

'Better leave them their cursed money too,' shouted another. 'It might be bewitched and all.'

When the last of them had gone, Mistress Skelton looked at her devastated home and garden, and groaned. 'Fancy our own people turning on us like that. They're as bad as the Scots.'

The boys were running everywhere trying to retrieve the fallen money.

'Come on in, it's going to rain next,' Mistress Skelton said. 'We'll have to tidy the garden another day.'

This time she barred the door firmly but hardly had she done so than a familiar voice said: 'Peace be to all here,' and she opened it again to find Brother John and Brother Dominic come to hear their version of the disturbance.

Mistress Skelton told them what had happened and ended: 'If I find that confounded parchment, father, it'll go on the fire right away, rest assured of that. Nobody's calling my husband a heretic!'

The monks both smiled at her vehemence.

'I'm sure Master Skelton's a good son of the Church, but he must learn not to keep strange papers in his house. Now, be sure you all go to Mass tomorrow morning and we'll come back and talk to you later in the day.'

But by morning everyone had other things to think about. The wind rose and the rain which had begun as a mere drizzle increased to torrents. It dripped down the stone chimney Mistress Skelton was so proud of—it was the only wall chimney in the whole village— and soon it was seeping through the holes Garath had made in the thatch. Then the gale made the holes bigger till the boys' attic became so uncomfortable they took their palliasses downstairs and slept in the kitchen.

In the morning the storm was still raging and everyone went to church muffled in their cloaks, cold and miserable. All through the service the noise of the tempest could be heard and occasionally there was a crash of falling masonry in the central tower as some of the stone-work was dislodged.

When they reached home they found Gowkie Graeme stretched out on the floor, drying himself like a great, wet dog before the fire. Although the joiner had helped him rebuild his shelter with strong new posts after the raid, it had been no protection against the storm.

Mistress Skelton stirred up the fire and heated some stew. While they ate Gowkie, who had been roaming about quite unconcerned by the weather, told them of all the damage he had seen. The window shutters had been ripped from many houses leaving the people exposed to wind and rain, for they had no glass in their windows. Fences, too, were down, and the roofs of some of the oldest cottages had suffered badly. A few families had even had their doors blown in. There was flood water over all the low lying land and it was believed a number of sheep had been swept away.

'That'll serve Flockmaster right!' said Robin vindictively.

Mistress Skelton shook her head reprovingly, 'You've just been to church this morning!' Then she asked Gowkie if Widow Thwaite's cottage was all right. Gowkie seemed to think so, for it stood in a slight hollow, sheltered by trees.

The storm continued. The wind and rain lashed the house without ceasing. Draughts came in from all directions making it impossible to keep warm. It was also dark and depressing because the window shutters had to stay tightly closed and you couldn't see to do much with only the glow of the fire and the flickering of a few rushlights.

The boys played marbles in front of the hearth or amused themselves with Robin's jousting knights. Mistress Skelton tried to settle to her spinning but was constantly jumping up to place dishes under the holes where rain was dripping through and making pools all about them.

'Oh, this is terrible!' she cried in exasperation, as she put her wooden bread-mixing bowl under yet another little new waterfall. 'As soon as the storm eases off the slightest bit we must try to mend the roof or we'll be flooded out.'

The boys expected Gowkie would help them—he played with their toys readily enough!—but he had a trick of coming and going as he pleased. So when the rain finally slackened sufficiently for them to venture out of doors, Gowkie just vanished on his own peculiar business.

They couldn't wait, for the sky was still

overcast and it might begin to pour again at any moment. Luckily the joiner kept a good stack of ready-cut rushes behind the cottage, so the boys each mounted a ladder, and Mistress Skelton who dare not climb up herself, handed them sheaves of rushes as they were required.

It was very unpleasant work for the thatch was wet and slippery from the rain. But the biggest problem was getting the rushes into place, for the wind was still blowing strongly, making it extremely difficult to hold on to the ladders and thatch at the same time. And the largest holes seemed always to be just beyond their reach.

'Oh, the foul fiend take it!' cried Robin as they struggled to tie down the first completed piece of thatching with a straw rope, 'we'll never get it done.'

'Oh, Robin! Robin! Is that any way to speak when Our Lady herself has sent you a helper?

The boys turned quickly—Robin almost falling from his ladder—and they looked down at Brother John's kind, worn face. 'Come down David, let me be up there instead.'

Mistress Skelton made a curtsy. 'Oh, father,' she protested '*you* can't do our roof. It wouldn't be right.'

'And why not?' asked the monk, holding out his calloused hands. 'Work is prayer, as I've often told you.'

David and Brother John changed places, and to the boys' delighted surprise Brother John turned out to be an expert thatcher. The job was soon done and then they went into the house where Mistress Skelton gave everyone a drink of butter-milk and some oatcakes she'd made that morning. They tasted of smoke from the smuts which had blown down the chimney but after their hard toil nobody minded that.

When they'd finished, Brother John told them that news of the travellers had been received. In spite of bad roads and having to make a wide detour to avoid the robbers, they'd safely reached their destination, and another message to say when they expected to start the return journey could be looked for at any time.

'So the only thing now,' said Brother John, smiling kindly at Mistress Skelton, 'is to find that mysterious parchment before it causes more trouble. I suppose you still haven't any idea where it could be?'

'Oh no,' Mistress Skelton was beginning, 'I've searched everywhere . . .'

'It's here!' interrupted a girl's voice, and they all looked round startled. Margery was pushing open the unbarred door. 'I'm sorry I couldn't come sooner.' She sounded rather breathless. 'I've had such a job to coax grandmother. She wouldn't let me out till I'd promised to run all the way—she's so afraid of trees falling on me.' Several villagers had been injured in this way in the storm.

Margery advanced into the room, and shaking back her tattered cloak, held out the long leather case.

'Why, child,' gasped Mistress Skelton, 'where *did* you find it?'

'Oh,' explained Margery coolly, 'I was hiding in the pig sty to see what happened, so when Garath put it on the wall, I just picked it up and went home. Grandmother was angry at first in case anyone had seen me and accused us of witchcraft, but I knew a place to keep it perfectly safe for you.'

'Where was that?' cried the boys together, and David added, 'Oh Margery, you were brave! Weren't you frightened of Garath?'

'Not of him finding it,' said Margery, 'because I put it in Esmerelda's nest. Even Garath daren't go near her now. You see, she won't let anyone but me touch her when she's broody.'

She sounded so proud of her pet they all burst out laughing, especially Brother John who was sitting in Master Skelton's armchair and nearly fell out of it in his mirth.

'Oh Margery! What a thing to think of! Surely the Blessed Saints inspired you!' He controlled himself with difficulty and held out his hand for the packet. As Margery gave it to him, they could see bits of white fluff sticking to it and one end bore definite traces of Esmerelda's sharp beak. It also had a most peculiar smell.

Brother John slowly opened the case and carefully unrolled the parchment, his features becoming graver as he studied it.

'What is it, father?' asked Mistress Skelton fearfully. 'Is it very wicked?' They were all trying to look at the strange, heavy writing.

'No, it's as I expected. Only a portion of the scriptures written in English.'

'Oh, Christ have mercy!' Mistress Skelton

115

crossed herself, 'then does that mean . . . '

'Now, don't worry too much yet, mistress,' said Brother John soothingly. 'It's certainly a very serious matter and one My Lord Abbot alone must deal with. But there's no proof Master Skelton hid the parchment in the thatch or that he ever read it. And if he had it might be no great matter if he only keeps quiet about it. My Lord Abbot knows a day will come—maybe—' murmured the monk half to himself—'sooner than we expect—when everybody in the land will be allowed to read it. But for the present we must all pray our very hardest that My Lord Abbot will graciously overlook Master Skelton's indiscretion . . . '

He blessed them and said to Margery, 'Come, my child, I'll see you safely home. I fear the storm has not blown itself out yet.'

Brother John was right about the weather. For two more days the wind howled and whined round the house and the rain battered against the shutters. But the repaired roof stayed whole, and during the third night the gale ceased as suddenly as it had begun, and in the morning they went out to a beautiful, sunny, clean-washed world.

After sitting in the dark house and worrying about things for so long, it was marvellous to be at liberty in the fresh open air again. Everything seemed to be new and bright. The birds were singing happily, the grass had grown greener, and all the plants were further out than when they'd last seen them.

Two trees had blown down on the common near the cottage, so the boys ran to climb on them while Mistress Skelton wandered thoughtfully round the garden inspecting her favourite plants.

The boys scrambled along the trunks of the trees and swung about in the branches, quite forgetting all their troubles for the moment till they suddenly saw Brother John coming towards the house.

They hurled themselves to the ground and pelted off to meet him.

'Peace be to you!' the monk beamed at them. 'Our prayers have been heard! Your father's safe now, Robin! But he'll not be returning for at least another week. A message came last night that he'd obtained some excellent quality timber and was staying to see it loaded on to the wagons, then he'll travel back with them. The parchment's been destroyed and My Lord Abbot is so pleased about the panelling he will say nothing more about the matter.'

'But Flockmaster,' asked David, 'won't he go on making trouble?'

'No,' Brother John assured him. 'Flockmaster and his family are going to one of our farms in the mountains. Brother Dominic is just telling them now. Perhaps digging sheep out of snowdrifts may help to cool their tempers. And as for the rest of the village, well, there's been a lot of damage done and I think they'll appreciate having a good craftsman like Master Skelton around again. So now, Robin, suppose you both go and tell Margery your good news. I must have a little talk with your mother—and Robin,' the monk caught Robin's arm as he was about to dash off in his usual impetuous way, and spoke rather sternly: 'don't ever forget what you owe to that child. With the blessing of Heaven she saved you from worse horrors than you realize.'

'Oh, father, I do know,' Robin answered quickly but sincerely. He had learnt a lot that stormy spring. 'Mother's been going on about it all these last few days. She says she'll think of Margery as her daughter from now on—just as we two are her sons—and she's going to do all kinds of things for Widow Thwaite—but come on, David.'

Hastily bowing their heads in response to the monk's blessing, the boys scampered off and met Margery half way between their two houses. She was carrying a bunch of newly picked primroses in her hand.

'Oh, isn't everything *wonderful*!' she cried in delight, when they'd told her what Brother John had said. 'Master Skelton isn't going to get into trouble, Garath's going away. It's spring at last—and Esmerelda has twelve goslings! Come and see them, both of you, right away!'

AUTHOR'S NOTE

The period dealt with in this book is the early sixteenth century, when people were beginning to question the authority of the church. The children in the story grew up to witness the dissolution of the great monastery which had ruled their lives for so long, and David grieved, as all true craftsmen must, that the new freedom had to be accompanied by the destruction of much that was old and beautiful.

But I like to imagine that when Robin fulfilled his ambition of going off to the wars, David stayed at home and married Margery, and his workshop became a place of refuge for the little children of the village whenever they were in any kind of trouble.

M.A. Wood is a writer and lecturer who lives near Carlisle. Her other historical novels for children are **When the Beacons Blazed** (also available from Byway Books) which is set on the Scottish side of the Border and features several of the same characters as in this story, and **Master Deor's Apprentice.**